FRED BERRY
DAVID HUTCHISON
ZOMBIE KID DIARIES
WALKING DAD
Sequel to the New York Times Bestseller
CUSTODY -AWARD-

FRED PERRY DAVID HUTCHISON
ZOMBIE KID DIARIES™
WALKING DAD
CUSTODY
-AWARD-

WALKING DAD

Writer - Fred Perry
Artist - David Hutchison
Inspiration & Concept - Brian Denham & Joe Dunn
Editors - Robby Bevard & Doug Dlin
Graphic Designer - Brian Denham
Cover Design - Brian Denham
Layout - Doug Dlin

***Zombie Kid Diaries* series**
Zombie Kid Diaries 1: Playing Dead
Zombie Kid Diaries 2: Grossery Games
Zombie Kid Diaries 3: Walking Dad

Also Available by the Author:
The Littlest Zombie Trade Paperback
PeeboManga 1.0

Come visit us online at
www.antarctic-press.com
Antarctic Press
7272 Wurzbach, Suite 204
San Antonio, TX 78240

ISBN: 978-0-9850925-7-3
Printed and bound in Canada.

Monday

Sunny all day.

Breakfast: I'm still trying to decide what it was, but it didn't go down without a fight!

Today's Record: *Atomic vs. Discom 3 Ultimate Arcade Edition 2012* (Man, that's a long name for a fighting game...) – 66 consecutive online wins, 20 perfects. I was seriously on a streak.

In case my previous journals all get consumed in a fire, or are seized by government secret agents attempting to gather some dirt on me, it's best if I start this new journal with a brief introduction.

I'm a middle school zombie named William Stokes. Everyone just calls me Bill. Nobody calls me a zombie. That's a secret.

BILL STOKES: ZOMBIUS KIDDIUS MIDDLESCHOOLIUS (IN LATIN SCIENCY SPEAK)

It's a secret that's not hard to keep, believe it or not. When I look in the mirror, I see the same face I had before Mom brought home that strange virus. She contracted it back when she was a paid volunteer for medicinal testing from six or seven different companies all at once.

I still look just like I looked last summer. Except maybe my hair is a bit stringy and my nails are a little long and hard. Maybe my teeth are a bit longer and duller. My skin's paler and more clammy, too. But that might also be puberty kicking in.

It seems zombies aren't all that noticeable until people are getting bitten. Not that I feel at all like biting people. Much.

I mean, it's true, my appetite's flipped on me. I smell things differently than before. While folks do smell like bakery goods, hot dogs and pizzas now, it's not like anyone's ready to bite into a pizza that's riding next to them on the city bus, right? Not while he's checking his email, anyway.

I've got enough common sense to not go around chewing on folks. No matter how good they smell or might taste, eating somebody's a sure way to get this secret of ours found out! Fortunately, I'm never really hungry—not for people. Mom was a great cook before she was a zombie, but she's an even better cook since!

Well, except this one time. I chewed on Steve, a bully at school, during lunch period. But that was a fight, and I was gnawing in self-defense, so that doesn't count. And there was this one other time at Camp Woodchunk where I snacked on this guy's fingers...but he was, like, long gone and departed and all beef-jerkied, so that doesn't count, either.

The only thing I have trouble with is finding ways to control the unfortunate side effects of eating Mom's zombie cuisine. And by unfortunate, I mean covering up skin disorders that disappear and reappear; controlling zits big enough to block out the sun; and, most importantly, keeping my stinky, toxic, unspeakably horrific zombie gas from ending all life on Earth as we know it.

I wish I were joking. If the government discovered my existence, they'd probably classify me as a WMD right then and there! Especially if they poked at my belly too hard!

Fortunately, I've developed a few technologies to handle my various temporary skin conditions, mega-zit outbreaks and, most importantly, Zombie B.O. The best defense so far has been baking soda. This stuff has saved me more often than I can count!

And I'll need all the help I can get if I'm going to make it through middle school in one piece. All I have to do is survive long enough for my future career as a world champion pro-gamer to kick into high gear.

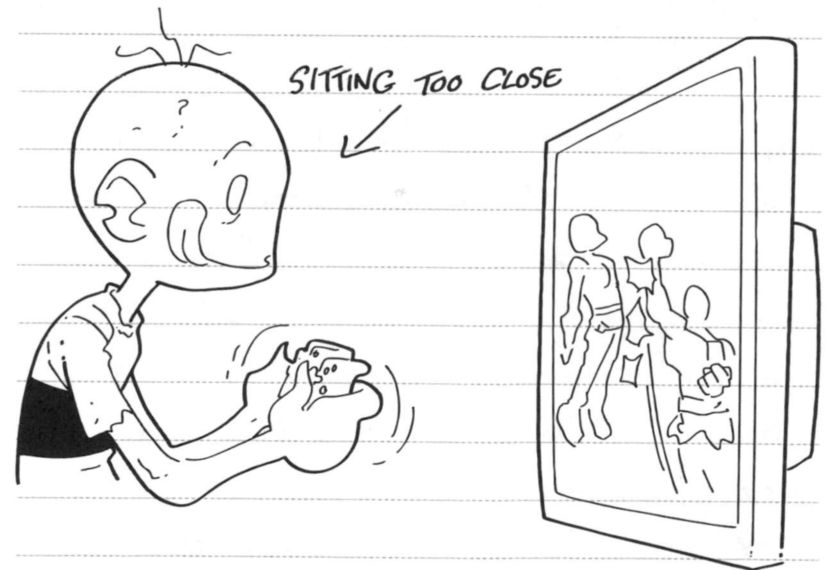

School was the same old routine today, except for one thing a little out of the ordinary. On the way to and from my bus stop, there was this powder-blue compact car that was just lurking on the corner about half a block away. The guy sitting in the car was reading a magazine or a newspaper, so I couldn't see who he was.

I have to keep my eyes out for this kind of stuff. Like I said before, the government would freak out if they discovered there were real zombies living it up in some suburb. If that guy is some CIA or FBI agent sniffing around for evidence, then I've got to be extra-careful! Tomorrow, if that blue compact is still lurking in that spot, I'm going to get Larry or Janine (more on them in a bit) to help me check things out!

Just thinking about that car made me nervous, though. To take my mind off it, I started thinking about studying. THAT's how desperate I was.

While browsing over the homework assignment, I checked my own records, then added up my grade point average. I'm kinda falling behind. I'll need a "B" on the midterm to keep things nice and dull, but not so dim that somebody decides to get me a tutor, which is worse than being shoved into an advanced placement course that would eat up all my free time. It's a pretty broad line between being adept and being a derp.

STAY IN THE "BUTTER ZONE!"
GEEK
NORMAL?
DERP
You still have to watch your step if you're clever enough to blend in to buck the system!
Overachieve and work like a dog for the rest of your life! It's fun!
Dur-hurr! Minimum-wage high school dropout careers be funnerer!!
SCIENCE
COLLEGE DEGREE
MATH
W
HI SKOL DROP OWT

I did some of the homework drills and then my own practice work to make sure I'd be familiar enough with the material to score a perfect one hundred. It's a lot easier to scale back your grade than to try to push it higher. Easy-mode American history is mostly who did what, where they did it, and when. To make it interesting, I made myself some comics about all the facts. I find you remember stuff better when you make fun of it.

"GREAT TROLLS OF AMERICAN HISTORY"
Pres. of 2nd Continental Congress, John Hancock is signing the Declaration of Independence in the summer of 1776!

Charles Johnson, witness to the signing, thought it would be funny not to tell John there were going to be 55 OTHER signatures in that "blank space".

By the time I was finished, I had a good forty minutes before bed for gaming. But if I stay up too long, Mom shuffles to the fuse box and shuts off the power. Even as a zombie, Mom is a bedtime dictator, and her word (or grunt) is law!

I signed online with my gamer tag, "Kid Dracula", and proceeded to whip the pants off of every poor sap in the *Atomic* vs. *Discom* challenge lobby! There were some high-level "pros" in the lobby too, and even THEY fell victim to the "KD" horror spree!

I mean, sure, I've gotten these crazy reflexes as a side effect of my new "zombie" status, and I've been using them to rocket me past the competition in all the local and online video game tournaments. But today was a little different. Today, I was on fire!

Maybe my adrenaline was still working overtime because I was anxious about that blue car and what might be a government extra-weird-files agent sniffing for paranormal entities...like me! I'm still a little nervous, to tell the truth. What if I'm taking out the garbage, and an FBI zombie-catching squad jumps out at me from the bushes? I've got my zombie reflexes and fast fingers, but after that surprise burst of speed, I'm as slow as a turtle! There's no way I can outrun a SWAT team!

UNLESS THEY'VE COME TO CHALLENGE ME TO A *SUPER SMASHER SISTERS*, I'M PRETTY MUCH HOSED IF THIS WERE TO HAPPEN!

Sure, Mom and I aren't gonna eat anybody (I think). All those years of zombie movies and video games will have people on edge, though. I can't afford to let down my guard, especially when it looks like someone I don't know has been nosing around for me!

You see, I've got plans for my future, and nothing's going to stop me—not even my "zombie" condition! Not only am I going to be a professional competitive gaming superstar, I'm going to be the best in the whole world! I'm more than good enough; I was top-notch even before I contracted that virus.

Like I said, now I've got some crazy reflexes and extra-nimble thumbs. This kind of makes sense. If a zombie and a normal person are rounding a blind corner and—bam—they surprise each other, who always reacts first? Who always gets the first jump? The zombie!

Fast fingers seem to be part of the deal, too. In the movies, once a zombie grabs someone, they stay grabbed nine times out of ten. Zombies are anything but butterfingers. The only major drawback seems to be everything that happens AFTER that initial surprise "jump". I'm a reeeeally slow runner, and my athletic coordination is that of a three-toed sloth's pet turtle.

My mind is still sharp... isn't it? I wonder if Mom's mind is still sharp too.
I don't have to blink anymore, and I can see in the dark reeeeally good, too.
My guts have changed! I don't need to eat all that much, but when I do, it makes it toxic.
Extra-nimble digits! I wonder if I can play the piano?

Hard work and super talent isn't everything. Preparation is key, and I always try to be prepared, especially in games. Especially in this "life career" game! That's where my journal entries come in.

Once I'm ready to take the limelight, these volumes can be used for the foundation of creating the perfect conditions for my perfect game sessions! A computer program will analyze my scores, the weather, what I ate, and what stress levels I had on any given day in the past.

AS GOOD AS GOLD, BABY!

With that data, I can easily get a solid analysis! Having data dating back from middle school to when I'm an old man at twenty-five will be the edge I need to make millions in the pro-gaming arena! And that arena will be an e-sport phenomenon just about the time I'm ready to be world champ!

Hope I can get some sleep tonight. I like being supercharged while playing online, but I don't like being jittery while I'm not! I hope I'm just imagining things!

Tuesday

Slight Overcast

Breakfast: Sun-dried flap-cats and syrup

Today's Record: No online scores. (You'll see why.)

I did mention my mom is a really good cook, right? Well, just the other weekend, the neighborhood fat tabby cat passed away right in our back yard! What a stroke of luck! For Mom, me, and our zombie appetites, that was like the pizza delivery guy, the ice cream man, and a fully cookie-laden girl scout all breaking down in front of our house, and then deciding, "To heck with it! Let's throw a party right here! Right NOW!"

AWWWW, MANNNN! WHAT DO WE DO NOW!?

WAIT! I KNOW! PARTY HARD!!!

Well, Mom's been coming up with new ways to serve the remains of the cat as delicious, nutritious meals! However, I'm one hundred percent sure they aren't fit for non-zombie consumption. Today's flap-cats were extra crispy on the outside and gooey-chewy on the inside! They reminded me of Mom's buttery, cream-filled waffles from the old pre-zombie days. Just good mood food! I almost forgot to neutralize the toxic gases with baking soda, though.

The thing is, I kind of feel guilty about chowing down on the cat now. I didn't realize until later that it was actually Janine's favorite neighborhood tabby cat, Sporky, and his disappearance kind of put the cherry on top of her cruddy day!

Janine's a classmate of mine, by the way. She's got the standard, annoying cuteness-obsession that girls have, but don't let that fool you! She can trade combos with the best of them online! She and Larry, my neighbor and friend since I was little, are still my video game tournament teammates. Though they don't have the online win records that I do, they don't exactly need me to carry them through a contest. Together, we make up "The Three Tricycles of the Apocalypse". There's me, "Kid Dracula". Janine is "SanReaper". Larry is "Darth Larry". We've entered six tournaments together since September, and we've swept every last one!

We meet at lunch to discuss our strategies for upcoming events, share hints, and just hang out. Larry and I were stoked about the new fighting game that just came out: *Street Battler versus Kentetsu*. (That's Japanese: ken = "fist", tetsu = "iron".)

I thought for sure Janine would be all about the cutesy gag characters she always tends to gravitate towards. But not this time. She was studying the fact sheets Larry printed out on "Chun Lethalina", the Wing Chun cybernetic ninja chick! WAY out of her normal line of interest!

IS JANINE FINALLY OVER HER CUTESY MANIA!?!

When we asked her about her not picking "Bubblie", the flower-power puffy girl, or "Flutterspark", the little unicorn boy, she replied that the world isn't all sunshine and rainbows, and that she had to start thinking tougher. That's when Larry and I learned what happened to Janine that morning.

NEVER IN A MILLION YEARS DID I THINK THIS WOULD HAPPEN!

Janine then opened her little rainbow-kitty purse and showed us her little rainbow-kitty can of mace. It was empty! She'd emptied it on some guy who drove up to her while she was on her way to the school bus stop. The guy was driving a powder-blue compact! He'd rolled right up to Janine and started asking weird questions about her and about us!

So, Janine did what any sensible kid should do when some strange, shady dude rolls up to get all nosy: She gave him a quick spritz and got the heck outta there!

There was a crossing guard near the bus stop, and when Janine made it to him, the car was long gone, but that whole ordeal must have really shaken Janine up. But even that wasn't what was really bothering her.

Janine hadn't noticed that the stranger's car was pulling up beside her because she was feeling really sad. Sporky was her favorite neighborhood tabby cat, and since that cat had never missed a meal before this weekend, Janine was worried sick.

She was certain that something had happened to it. As a matter of fact, she was sure Sporky was gone forever. She could "feel it in her heart."

Just then, my tummy rumbled. And rumbled. And RUMBLED! It was as if Sporky was calling out to Janine, "HELP! Bill had me for his cheeseburger!"

I never felt that guilty before! Never in my entire life!

That would have been the end of that, if only Sporky'd rested in peace, but he didn't.

Every time we tried to start a brand new conversation, my stomach rumbled—a nice, loud rumble that even made one of the kids passing by our table stop and to ask, "What the heck was that?!"

I tried thumping my tummy with my palm a little bit. "Indigestion," I said. But, I'm telling you, Sporky just would not shut up! Every few minutes, it was "Growl! Growl! GROWL!" My stomach growls got so loud that they were impossible to pretend to ignore. So loud that I had come up with a reason behind all the noise. But I panicked. I should have said that I ate a really bad burrito last night. I should have said I made a mistake and ate some stale frozen pizza and it was coming back on me. I should have said WHAT I ate.

Instead, I said "Musta been something I ate." Big mistake. It gave Harold just the tiniest room to make one of his stale jokes. "You musta swallowed a dog to catch the cat to catch the bird to catch the spidah that wiggled and jiggled and tiggled inside yah!" That made Janine look right at me, smile weirdly and ask, "Swallowed a cat?"

When Janine looked at me, I could see in her eyes the question flashing into her head for just a brief instant. She involuntarily cocked her head to the side and arched an eyebrow. I could just read it on her face as she mentally asked herself, "Does Bill, or his stomach, have anything to do with poor Sporky's disappearance?" Thank goodness I've been practicing my poker face!

At that very moment, my stomach growled AGAIN, as if Sporky were crying out to her, "Yes! Bill did it! I'm in here!!!" It was like that Edgar Allen Poe story "The Tell Tale Heart" or something!

Fortunately, plausible deniability can pull even the most guilty fat out of the hottest fire! Instead of hiding the truth, I put it out there in plain sight, confessing everything in the most sarcastic way possible! "Yes, Janine, I'm a zombie horror just like in the movies, and

I crave the sweet, delicious flesh of neighborhood alley cats!"

That got Janine to blush and apologize for being silly. "I just miss Sporky. He was a good kitty." So, I was off the hook, but man, did I feel guilty! I still do! But there's no way I'm ever going to make it up to her if my zombieness is exposed to the world!

It's not as if Sporky was alive before Mom put him in the fridge. We were just recycling! Yeah! That's exactly what we were doing! It's just too bad that I can't tell my friends and make them understand!

As soon as my stomach calmed down, I took the chance to change the subject by asking if they'd caught the guy who'd stalked Janine. No such luck, but when Janine told me about the questions she was asked, there could be no doubt! That stalker was CIA or FBI, and he was looking for information on ME!

He asked if my Mom had any boyfriends coming around the house. He asked if our circle of friends included anyone else besides me, Janine and Larry. He asked about our Sunday night meetings. No wonder Janine is feeling like cutesy time is over and wants to pick a butt-kicking ninja gal for her avatar!

So yeah, I feel bad for Janine and totally guilty because everything is my fault! First, Mom and I eat her favorite pet. Then, I cover it up.

THEN, she's interrogated by some weirdo who might turn out to be a special agent from the FBI's paranormal files! I'll have to find a way to make it up to her!

The whole thing got me too shaken up to practice straight away, so I just wrote in my diary and did some more of my history comics. Here's one I copied from my class notebook. Maybe the computer program that will analyze my diaries will be able to use THIS as data too!

YET ANOTHER INSTALLMENT OF
"GREAT TROLLS IN AMERICAN HISTORY: WAR OF 1812 RESULTS!

After that, I felt like playing again. So I signed in, but saw Janine was in the *Atomic vs. Discom* lobby, and she was having a really awesome winning streak. I watched some of her games and saw she was using this kick-butt, all-tough-gal team of wreckers: She-muscle, Blazebird and Batcatta! Janine was tearing up everybody with that trio! I think she was working out some stress, and I really didn't feel like goin' in and ruining her rampage. So I signed out and practiced offline.

See? I'm nice sometimes.

Wednesday

Sunny in the morning, rainy in the evening.

Breakfast: Cracklin' Curdle Flakes and rancid juice! (YUM!)

Today's Record: *Atomic vs. Discom 3 Utimate Arcade Edition 2012* – 34 consecutive online wins, 8 perfects.

I woke up this morning because my new cell phone buzzed me awake with a text from Mom.

Yeah, we got cell phones now. Mom got them from MalMart, where she works as a front door greeter and shoplifter tackler.

SHE'S ACTUALLY A THREE-TIME EMPLOYEE OF THE WEEK NOW!

We're zombies with call plans!

The text read, "Bill, get up, get showered and dressed. I set out your blue shirt. I still can't iron, so you'll have to take care of that yourself. I've forwarded a list of chores I want you to take care of when you get home from school today! Love, Mom."

From her text messages, I've learned that Mom's still in there, after all. It took her some time to get the knack of our zombie thumb dexterity, but she can twiddle like a pro now. Almost as good as I can, actually! Too bad our wrists, elbows, knees, shoulders and hips are still so klutzy!

THESE DAYS, THIS IS BASIC MOTHER/SON COMMUNICATION FOR NORMAL PEOPLE TOO, ISN'T IT?

I've got mixed feelings about this, though. On the one hand, I don't have to worry as much about her state of mind. That's a BIG relief! On the other hand, I can't pretend I don't understand what she wants from me when, for instance, she shoves a soapy dishcloth in my face and grunts her "Get to work on those dishes" zombie-mom grunt!

WHHHHhhnmshTHNNG
DSHHMNGHH!!!

Wash the daisies?!!

After breakfast, I thought about asking Mom about our condition, but I didn't really know how to ask her. She seemed to be avoiding the question too. I was just relieved we could communicate again, you know? I didn't even mind the threat of her nagging about me coming straight home from school to do chores, but I know that'll get old fast.

I left the house and took my shortcut to the bus stop, as per usual. But I was so wrapped up in my phone that I didn't even notice the blue compact right at the corner!

Janine got there about the same time I did. SHE noticed! She grabbed the crosswalk guard and pointed out that car to him. The guard got out his phone and dialed 911, but before he could finish, the car peeled out!

By the time a police car got on the scene, we were leaving on the bus. Janine wanted to stay to talk to the cops, but the crosswalk guard said he'd handle it. She still had her hand in her rainbow-kitty purse when she sat with me and Larry, who'd gotten a few blocks ahead of us. I know she had another can of rainbow-kitty mace ready for action. Man, don't mess with Janine! When she's out of cutie-mascot-fangirl mode, she's dangerous!

The "Bitts-Maru" hair clip, her trademark accessory. Seems like she has one for all occasions.
These eyes go gaga over ponies and glitter, but are still sharp enough to spot a scrub player missing a link!
Go ahead... Make. My. Day!
OHAYO
A "Hiya Kitty" backpack with "good morning" in Japanese on it. I think it's an import, but they kept the name for *Kentetsu* the same, so who knows?
A can of rainbow-kitty mace. I'm more surprised that Sanrita even MAKES this stuff than I am that Janine always carries it.

The midterm was today, and it was breezier than I expected. I think I messed up and got an "A", though. My rumbling tummy signified urgent biological needs and totally derailed my concentration, so I rushed through the test without checking to make sure I had enough of the answers wrong.

I don't take chances with MY gas. Even the slightest hint of a fart is a huge emergency for me. Seriously. With my guts and and my diet, the desolation I could cause is truly a frightening thought. In that arena, I honestly believe I outclass every fictional "monster" out there!

It was a false alarm. I was afraid I hadn't taken enough baking soda, but I did. Just a little, harmless burp came out from the stomach rumble. But something strange caught my attention on my way back to class: I saw a room down the hall emptying out, a room in the upperclassmen section! Everyone was yelling and fussing and holding their noses! Some kids were even upchucking as they fled from the room and out into the hall! Somebody'd farted HARD in that room! And that somebody was Steve!

Steve was my personal demon during the first semester. A bully of the classic variety, he did everything he could to make my scholastic experience a flippin' nightmare!

But recently, he's left me and everyone else alone. Now, he seems to be some kind of geek that keeps to himself in the lunchroom. I've been wondering what he's been up to, but I couldn't bring myself to care enough to investigate. I'd heard a rumor that he gets his lunch from the pet shop these days. He probably developed a taste for the disgusting snack food he made all the kids in the lunchroom eat back when he was pranking everybody.

His new snack food was probably the source of that gas attack. I guess gross food makes gross gas, whether you're a zombie or a normal kid!

When I got home, I got a text from Mom reminding me to do those chores. To tell the truth, the lawn did need a trim. After I was done, I got up enough courage to text Mom a question about us.

"Mom, are we really zombies? Are we dead?" Mom had been quick to answer any text I'd sent that morning and afternoon, but for that one, I had to wait.

"We're not dead. We're not hurt. But we're not the same." A little bit later, she texted, "I'm still your mom. You're still my Bill. That's enough for me. Wash up for dinner. I caught another squirrel. <3"

And that squirrel pot pie was scrumdelicious!!!

Later on, I signed in for more practice with *Atomic vs Discom 3*. I gotta say, Janine was on fire again! She almost won a set! And it was impossible to score a "perfect" against her! Larry needs to step it up because, Janine is leaving him in the dust! This Sunday, during our team practice sessions, I'm going to try to coach Larry on his mix-ups and trap-making. He's too nice. He needs to get the same "eye of the tiger" that Janine now sports!

Thursday
Cloudy all day
Breakfast: "Beak-fast" burritos
Today's Record: No gaming tonight

Man, what an awful day! What made it worse was that it totally ruined the good mood Mom's breakfast put me in. "Beak-fast" burritos, made "fresh" from the grackles that nest in the tree out back! The grackles are fried, rolled in warm, moldy, baked tortillas and grilled with the grease for topping! Mmm, mmmm, GOOD! They remind me of the "pigs-in-a-blanket" breakfast food I had back in the old days, but with extra butter and blueberry syrup, and with crunchy bacon added inside!

DOESN'T IT MAKE YOUR MOUTH WATER!?!

So, I was blissfully on my way to the bus stop with a full and happy tummy, when out of nowhere came that powder-blue car! Janine was there, and so was the crosswalk guard, but before anyone could do anything, the car door opened, and out came MY DAD! Of all the people in the whole wide world, he was the last person I would have ever suspected to be behind that wheel! Talk about a blindside!

The last time I saw Dad, he was being hauled away to prison for setting fire to our old house for the insurance. My last memories of our times together are of him yelling at Mom and me for stupid stuff just because he got fired from his investment banker job for cheating and stealing. Even with the zombie virus, things were much, MUCH nicer around the house with him away in jail. But now he's out!?!

DEADBEAT DAD PROFILE
NAME FRANK STOKES:
TAGS: INVESTMENT FRAUD, BULLYING, YELLING AT MOM FOR NO REASON, THROWING A SHOE AT ME 'CAUSE I SPILLED HIS MILK BY ACCIDENT, CALLING MOM AND ME LOSERS OVER AND OVER, ARSON, SCAMMING, BAD AT VIDEO GAMES AND A SORE LOSER!

I should have pretended I didn't know him. I should have told the crosswalk guard to call the cops again. But I was so shocked, I just blurted out "Dad!?!" As SOON as I said it, I realized the mistake I'd made! Janine and the crosswalk guard immediately turned to me and said, "Ooooh! He's your father! Oh! Okay, false alarm!"

Gah! I'm so STUPID!

Dad played it up like he was all friendly. He told everyone that he's back from being away for a while, and that he was just making sure I was okay and was seeing the right friends. I couldn't say anything, I was so shocked! I was trying to get my mouth to say "No," but Dad was right there and I was...

I was scared!

UGH! I CAN'T BELIEVE JANINE BOUGHT THAT NICE ACT!

That's when Janine started apologizing for spraying Dad in the face! I sooo wanted to tell her not to be sorry and that she could spritz Dad with a FLAME THROWER for all I cared, but I couldn't snap out being stunned! Not until he was gone and I was on the bus!

Janine was back in blissful rainbow-kitty land again, and that made me realize Dad had already made a good impression on everybody. Especially Janine, who was now relieved she wasn't being stalked by a maniac! I'd forgotten that Dad could slather on the charm when he wanted to get someone to trust him. That's how he got all those investors hooked when he was running that scam that got him fired from his firm! Dad's got Dracula's hypno powers!

Even at lunch, Janine couldn't stop saying sorry for blasting my dad with pepper spray! I couldn't take it anymore, and instead of the careful explanation I was coming up with all morning, I just blurted out "Dad's a jerk! And if you want to mace him again, be my guest!"

As I knew she wouldn't, Janine didn't believe me. That nice-guy act had her hook, line, and sinker! Larry wasn't much better off, either. Since he'd moved from our old cul de sac to our new neighborhood before I did, he wasn't around for when our house burned down. So even HE couldn't believe "such a nice guy who was just looking out for me" was really a stone-cold scam artist!

I told them all about the night he got hauled away for arson, but Janine argued that it must have been a mistake because he's free now. As if bad guys never get out on a technicality! Janine said she'd loan me one of her rainbow-kitty comics in her collection because it dealt with "parental estrangement". Larry said he could find some info online on how to cope with my dad's return. I don't need a middle school support group! I need my friends to take my word when I say my dad's a skunk!

I tried and tried to explain how he scams people! I tried to explain that he's always after—

He's always after something. What is he after? Mom and I don't have anything HE'D want. Why'd he come back? What's his angle? He's up to something, or even if he got out of jail, he wouldn't be bothering with a pair of so-called "losers" like Mom and me.

Holy horseshoes, it was even worse than I thought! Today, he followed me home from the bus stop! He knows where we live! Dang it! I was always so careful before! I always checked to see if that blue car was around before I took my shortcut home! Some intense stuff just went down, and the neighbors might be calling the police on us! Hopefully, I can jot this all down before they take us away in the paddy wagon!

You see, there was a knock at the door, and when I answered it, I forgot to get a peek at the caller through the peep hole. Instead, I just turned the knob and pulled like an idiot. I was expecting Larry or Janine, the only folks who'd come around here at all before now. What I got was Dad shoving his foot in the door and slinking his way in where he definitely wasn't wanted!

He was all, "How you doin', Billy-boy!? Is your mother home?" smiling that smirky grin of his. It was the same grin he'd used to charm everyone at the bus stop.

"Go get your mother, Billy-boy. We gotta talk!" That's when Mom shuffled past the foyer on her way to the living room. Her face was buried in her phone, as she was busy texting someone, when she looked up and noticed Dad. Man, if I was shocked, Mom was horrified!

HOW DO YOU SHOCK A ZOMBIE MOM? HAVE HER EX-HUSBAND DROP BY UNEXPECTEDLY TO "CHAT"!

Dad just went right to Mom like he wanted to hug or something, but when Mom bared her teeth and snarled like a primal werewolf at him, he abandoned that idea!

He was still pressing his luck when he said, "Nadeen, they let me out of prison when I appealed. Lack of evidence! We can all be together again! Yeah, that's the ticket."

Dad's got this really bad habit of saying, "Yeah, that's the ticket," ESPECIALLY when he's nervous and he's lying. That's probably what contributed to him getting caught in that investment banker scam in the first place. But that crud doesn't work on me, and it really doesn't work on Mom! We've both got lie detectors for HIS bull!

Before Dad could say another word, Mom started yelling the most gosh-awful zombie-mom swear words at him! I had to cover my ears, they were so harsh!

Grahmmgfughh ghmhahghgx yushmfughshbakgggkkk!!!

I DON'T KNOW IF DAD KNEW WHAT MOM SAID, BUT I SURE DID!!!

At first Dad looked confused! But then he smirked that smirky smile of his and asked, "Nadeen? Have you been drinking? Wait until Child Protective Services hears about THIS!"

That burned Mom up! She pointed a finger at the door and roared like the lead singer of a death metal band—if that lead singer happened to be a *T. rex* from the Jurassic era!!!

MOM WOULD PWN AT A BATTLE OF THE METAL BANDS CONTEST!!!

The only other time I've heard a wrathful Mom-howl of that magnitude was one Christmas at Larry's back at our old cul de sac. Larry thought it would be a good idea to use a hibernating hornet's nest as a Christmas tree decoration, and his mom nearly woke the dead when she found out—the HARD WAY!

I BET THOSE TWO WOULD MAKE THE BEST METAL DUET OF ALL TIME!

Every dog in the neighborhood joined in the chorus and bayed, though the moon was a good five hours away from rising. I guess they figured Mom knew something that THEY didn't! Or they were scared that they would get in trouble if they didn't sound off too!

The color drained from Dad's face super fast! He gave this girly, high-pitched yelp that nearly harmonized with Mom's roar!

I could tell by the way he ran out of the house that Dad was just barely holding his fudge too!

No cops came by despite the noise. I guess the neighbors were okay with just one scream from the depths of horror and then silence! The peace is only really disturbed when things are continually disturbing, it seems. Just like that old joke: No one would want to see a kindly old shade tree in the park chopped down if that tree could scream. But everyone would love to see a kindly old shade tree in the park chopped down if that tree screamed ALL THE TIME!

I'm hoping I've seen the last of Dad, but I know I haven't. And now that he's snooping around, it's going to be tougher than ever to keep our zombieness under wraps. Mom texted me before bed. I thought she might be mad at me for opening the door for Dad by mistake, but the message just read, "Don't worry about Frank. Your Mother will handle HIM from now on."

That made me feel a lot better, but I was still too nervous to sign online and play tonight.

Instead, I decided to start a little project to cheer Janine up a little. I'd been going through her HeadBook photo gallery to gather all the info I could on Sporky, and it seemed she's taken pics of that kitty ever since Sporky was a little ball of fluff! So now I could draw a few cartoons as a memento or keepsake. It wasn't that hard to think of cartoon strips, either, because Sporky was a pretty doofy kitty. That's probably why Janine liked him so much.

After I drew the images, I scanned and sent them to her email account.

She sent me back an email with what seemed like four hundred smiley faces, so I guess she liked them!

Friday

Sunny

Breakfast: My all-time favorite! Stale Frosted Sugar Tufts!

Today's record: Street Battler vs, Kentetsu – 25 consecutive wins, 18 perfects

No sign of Dad all day today. I'm still a little nervous, but hopeful. Maybe he took the hint and decided to get out of our lives before Mom bites his face off. She could do it, too! Whatever changed us also made our jaws and teeth a lot better at chomping stuff. At least, I'm guessing that's what's going on. I know for a fact I was never able to bite all the way through an old ham bone before! Before this virus hit me, it took a few nibbles to even get through a carrot stick!

The good news is that Larry and Janine finally came over to my side about Dad being nothing but a jerk! It seems that they both had a run-in with him last night after he fled the scene from Mom scaring the bees out of him. Janine was with Larry and his parents at the MalMart, buying a copy of *Street Battler vs. Kentetsu*. They said Dad was buying a video game system and being a total Jerkenstein to the clerk, who was trying to help him with his expensive purchase.

The clerk was trying to tell Dad that he needed two controllers if he wanted to play a two-player game, and that he'd need to buy a second controller. Dad was yelling at him and calling him a loser! (His favorite insult. Believe me, I know.)

Dad was being a cheapskate, trying to scam and bully his way into them giving him a controller. Typical. But when Larry came over to help the clerk explain to Dad that he really did need two controllers, Larry got yelled at too. Real mean-like. What a jerk!

That's when Larry's parents came over. They're both nice people. Except you don't want to rile Larry's mom! (And you really don't want to screw up her Christmas tree with a hornets' nest.) Dad, true to form, saw that the odds were turning against his favor and switched to faker-mode to weasel his way out of the trouble he'd gotten himself into. I'm so glad both of my friends were there to witness the truth. I didn't rub it in...much.

I hate to say I told you so....
buuuuuuuuuuuuUUUUUUUhhhhhhtttt....

ACTUALLY, I DIDN'T HATE IT. IT FELT PRETTY DARN GOOD!!!

The only side effect to them seeing the light is Janine switching again into super-serious, no-nonsense mode! First, she advised me to have Mom file for a restraining order against Dad. Then, she flicked open her rainbow-kitty smart phone and started surfing for info on Dad's court case. By the end of lunch, she had forwarded me a whole mess of files and links! In just a few minutes, we all had a ton of dirt on Dad! Sheesh! Remind me never to get on HER bad side.

OBJECTION!

JANINE MCCLAIN,
ATTORNEY AT LAW

It seems Dad is at the center of a huge insider trading scandal, which basically means he was cheating on Wall Street. When everybody got caught, it was like a big game of musical chairs, and everybody found a seat to cover their butts in except Dad!

That still doesn't explain what Dad wanted with Mom and me. Janine said she'd look into it, and Larry said that his uncle is a lawyer and that he'd give me his number to give to Mom. I gotta admit, my friends are pretty awesome once they get going in the right direction. I almost feel guilty about the I-told-you-so's, but I DID tell them so!

MY PALS ROCK! IF I EVER LOSE CONTROL AND FIND MYSELF GOING ON A PEOPLE-EATING ZOMBIE RAMPAGE WHERE I CAN'T STOP CHOMPING FOLKS, I'M GOING TO DO MY BEST TO MAKE SURE I EAT THEM LAST!

The only downside for today was the results on the midterm. I did good. I did too darned good! Mr. Epstein, our American history teacher, held up the best midterm exam in the whole grade level: mine. The thing is, he was especially proud of the little cartoon that I'd doodled on the back of the exam! Crud! I thought I'd drawn that on another random sheet of paper! It was a strip of my "Great Trolls of American History" comic!

GREAT TROLLS OF AMERICAN HISTORY!!!

PRESIDENTIAL TROLL WIN!!!

He said they're going to run that stupid doodle in the next school paper, and that was that! At least I got Mr. Epstein to agree to let it run anonymously.

To make things even worse, guess who showed up AGAIN? Yeah, Dad! He was back, and with Child Protective Services and the cops! Mom answered the door this time. She had to let everybody in.

When I came downstairs and saw that Dad was with a social worker and a policewoman, I was real nervous! I thought for sure the jig was up and they'd take me away from Mom forever. I was scared! I was real scared! I almost started to cry! Why was Dad messing with us!? What could he possibly stand to gain by bringing in the authorities like this!?

I gotta admit, though, Mom played it cool! The surprise had worn off from the first time Dad visited, and she was apparently ready for this. She whipped out her cell phone and, get this, started typing out a message for the CPS guy! She was super fast, too! Once she was done, she handed the CPS guy the phone, and her message changed his expression from stern to sympathetic and supportive.

He said, "Awww! You're a parent with a disability! This explains everything!"

Mom gave him the doe-deer eyes and mumbled, "MmmmHmmm." Then she hugged me. Sorta. I helped out and hugged back! From that hint, Mom was hoping I'd play along, and I'm pretty sure I exceeded her expectations!

"Since Dad burned our house down, it's been just Mom and me. We're doin' the best we can, mister! But now he's back for some reason, and he won't leave us alone! Why are the cops and CPS on HIS side!?!"

I might have laid it on a little thick, but they bought everything, hook, line, and sinker! The guy from CPS and the lady cop gave Dad the meanest looks I'd ever seen a grown-up get by far! Man, did we flip the script on Dad!

All the "but, but, buts" in the world couldn't help Dad's case then. The CPS guy gave the house a quick scan. Everything was tidy thanks to the chores Mom made me do. (Whoa. I'm actually glad for those chores for once.) He looked at Dad again in total disgust then said, "False alarm. We're done here." And that was the end of that! Except...that CPS guy? He stayed behind to text a message, then gave Mom's phone back.

Before leaving, he straightened his tie and said, "Mrs. Stokes, we're awfully sorry for this misunderstanding, and I personally feel that you are one of the bravest parents I've met in my career. If there's anything you need..."

And then he held up his hand to his ear like he was holding a phone. Then his eyes narrowed kinda seductive-like.

"...call me."

That CPS guy hit on my mom! My zombie-mom!!! I looked at her, and she wasn't objecting! She nodded and sorta smiled! Weeeeiiiiiird!

We were both relieved when everyone was gone. I tried to high-five Mom, but her wrists don't work too good, so she missed. Instead, we settled down to some leftovers as a victory dinner! Hopefully THAT is the last we'll see of Dad!

After dinner, I hurried over to Harold's for some quick games of *Street Battler vs. Kentetsu* before dark. Well, "hurried" as fast as I can move, anyway. Plus I wanted to scan the street for signs of Dad's car. Nope, he was gone. And my win streak, given the limited daylight I had to work with, was pretty sweet!

Sometimes things fall apart just to rearrange into an even better configuration!

Saturday

Overcast in the morning, but it cleared up by noon.
Breakfast: Skipped it. Too nervous to eat.
Today's Record: *Street Brawler vs. Kentetsu* – 65 consecutive wins, 2 perfects.

This morning was mostly chore work. Mom texted me at the crack of dawn, and she all but ordered me to help her get the house spic and span. Now, normally, I would have complained, but not today. I knew why she was on this super-cleanliness kick: We had to be ready in case Dad decided to try once more for whatever it is he's after. At this point, him getting the better of us by using the authorities or something isn't likely.

But I was right with Mom on this one. Let's cover our bases, then we can sit back and wait for that restraining order to finish processing.

After chores, I went upstairs to focus on messing up my homework. Why? Because I totally screwed up when I got that A-plus-plus on my midterm! Mr. Epstein thinks I'm a genius or something because he totally got into that little comic I did. He asked for my American History notebook after class on Friday, and I, in a classic brain-dead move, GAVE it to him, knowing full well that my other dumb comics were in there too. I should have just pretended I left it at home or something. I should have pretended it got eaten by a rabid pack of paper-hungry honey badgers!

He found and read all my "Great Trolls of American History" comics and was convinced that they should be published! He asked me to make six more of them so that he could collect them for a pamphlet to show to other teachers and a book publisher! That's my homework assignment!

So here I am, trying to find a way to prove that those "brilliant" 15 comics I did were nothing but flukes. And that's kind of tricky. I've already proven I know my facts by the content in those comics. What I've got to prove is that my humor is annoying, boring and unfit for scholastic consumption! I've gotta do the American History Trolls that NO ONE wants to see.

Let's try this one!

AT VALLEY FORGE, MAJOR JAMES MONROE TRICKED HIS WHOLE COMPANY INTO COMING TO LISTEN TO GENERAL WASHINGTON READ FROM THOMAS PAINE'S "THE AMERICAN CRISIS". THEY THOUGHT THEY WERE COMING TO HEAR GEORGE DO HIS FAMOUS "I CANNOT TELL A LIE!" STAND-UP COMEDY ROUTINE!

And there you go. Want to totally kill a joke? Bring Thomas Paine into the picture! He wrote a mess of political pamphlets that just kept getting him in trouble. Seriously, that guy didn't know when to let well enough alone! I'm going to mix him into my next five comics somehow. He annoyed the heck out of everyone in the eighteenth century, so why not drag his bones out from the dresser drawer they buried him in for one last engagement?

THOMAS PAINE! TROLLIN' FROM BEYOND THE GRAVE!

I stayed up in my room all night to work hard on this project. No way I'm taking chances with my future pro-gamer champion career. That seemed fine with Mom, because she said she was going out for about two hours. I assumed it was to get her cappuccino and CosMom magazine again, since it's Saturday. She still has her routine, and not even the virus has altered it. Meanwhile, I got the house locked down airtight! You know...just in case. Once I'd finished these annoying-by-design comics, I got right back to this diary.

Mom had a real surprise for me when she came home! You'll never believe who came over with her! Mr. Evans, the CPS social worker who gave Mom the googly eyes yesterday! Mom didn't go out for her magazine, she went out on a flippin' LUNCH DATE! After they came back, they sat downstairs texting each other at the dining table! I couldn't even eavesdrop! Except every now and then Mr. Evans chuckled all macho-like...and Mom kinda horse-giggled.

HERE'S ONE FOR THE "WEIRD DATING-MOM" RECORD BOOKS, FOLKS!

There was one thing—every so often, Mr. Evans would talk instead of text. I guess he's not as fast as Mom is. And I did hear him say that he's off our particular case. He said it was a "conflict of interest issue". Great. Way to go, Mom! You neutralized one of the people on our side against Dad! Well, maybe it doesn't matter anymore. If a social worker is dating my Mom, how could Dad possibly make a case that Mom's not a fit parent?

I'm guessing that's what Dad was after. He wants Mom declared as an unfit parent. But that means Dad's after...he's after ME? What could I possibly mean to Dad? Mom divorced him while he was in jail. She didn't want his alimony. What the high-def heck could he have wanted with ME?

I signed in online to practice, but my heart wasn't really into it this time. I didn't lose a single round, but I didn't score too many perfects, either. I guess I won't be getting my mind into the game again until all this turmoil's resolved.

Sunday

Sunny all day.

Breakfast: Pillbug cobbler. (Scraped fresh from the backyard lawn!)

Today's Record: *Street Battler vs, Kentetsu* – 20 consecutive wins, 11 perfects

Good old Mom, always trying new goodies! This time, it was extra delish! I knew it would be while she was making breakfast. Those little pillbugs were lively and squirmy in that mixing bowl, let me tell you! I snuck a handful and chewed 'em down like raisins. But I was cheating myself.

THESE ARE GOOD ON THEIR OWN, BUT MOM KICKS IT UP A NOTCH BY ADDING HER SPECIAL "MYSTERY CHUNK MAPLE SYRUP"!

They tasted okay fresh from the lawn, but they really delivered the flavor when Mom seared them in her iron skillet. Pecans never tasted that sweet and crunchy! If they ever find a cure for our condition, I'm really gonna miss all this great-tasting grossness!

While Mom kept herself busy with her texts to Mr. Evans, I went off to attend team practice at Janine's house. The main goal for this session was supposed to be about getting Larry up to speed with the rest of us.

Instead, it turned out to be a debrief on what Dad was doing Saturday, thanks to the evidence Janine gathered with her little rainbow-kitty smart phone's camera!

Janine's shots were taken from around a corner while using her phone to peek without being seen. And they were all pretty weird! It was shot after shot of Dad behind a grocery store or some place with huge dumpsters. In some of the shots, he was actually dumpster diving! His loot must have been carried off in the large, black duffle bags he brought with him.

WHAT IN THE WORLD IS HE UP TO?

Janine wanted me to copy all of the images from her smart phone onto mine, but my device didn't have enough memory. Since this is some kind of urgent mission for her, Janine loaned me her phone so I could bring the evidence to Mom personally. There were tons and tons of shots, I can see why she didn't just email them.

That, and Janine suspected Dad might even be shifty enough to hack into Mom's email account. Okay, Janine had me there. I gotta get Mom to change her password from "1234567" to something a little more secure, and I've gotta do that TODAY!

Larry's cell phone had enough room to back up the evidence, but he didn't copy it. He said that he was meeting his uncle on Monday at his uncle's law firm to see if there was any progress on the restraining order stuff. But all those pictures proved was that my Dad could be a into recycling or bottle collecting, so Larry didn't bother with 'em.

It was nice that my friends were helping me out with everything, but it still kind of derailed our practice session. We only got a little bit of coaching in for Larry, but it was enough for him to improve...slightly. Thankfully, there isn't another tournament for a while, so that can slide this time. I went home to practice and write in my diary after that.

Hopefully, after Larry's uncle hooks Mom up with that restraining order, the deadbeat dad disruptions to my life will finally come to an end!

Monday

Cloudy.

Dinner: Fried Chicken, green beans and mashed potatoes. Fresh apple pie.

Today's Record: None.

Yeah, something's wrong. You can tell just from that "dinner" entry, can't you? Well, you're right. Something went wrong. Horribly, horribly wrong.

Everything was pretty much business as usual this morning. I went to school. Mom went to her job at MalMart. I turned in my American History "homework", which Mr. Epstein seemed too busy to read. Or maybe he was just out of it because the coffee maker in the teacher's lounge broke down. Still, everything seemed pretty routine.

Little did I realize the horror that awaited me at home after school!

While walking home from the bus stop, I saw a police car, Dad's blue car, and a white sedan from CPS in our driveway. Out on the lawn, Dad was talking to a woman who must have been the new social worker assigned to the case. The front door was open, and the policemen were wheeling out our fridge on a big, orange hand truck! Evidence!

When I thought about what everyone might assume if they had opened that fridge to see all the "goodies" inside, my heart stopped in my throat!

Dad spotted me and ran up to me with his fake concerned voice. "Bill! Son! What has that woman been forcing you to eat? What has that woman been forcing you to do!?" He grabbed me hard and hugged me. When he did, I remembered those two black duffle bags from the pictures Janine took yesterday!

Son of a gun! He must have filled those bags with rotting garbage from the dumpster and was planning to put it in our fridge to frame us! But he didn't have to! If he'd jimmied the lock to get to our fridge, he would have discovered gross stuff already in there!

When he hugged me. I swear I could hear him chuckle. My dad is the world's biggest dork!!!

Mom got home slightly late, and Mr. Evans was with her. I think they'd had another little date or something. But even Mr. Evans couldn't help us out that time. He tried his best to calm Mom down, but she was ready to chew Dad's head off this time! Lucky for us, she listened to Mr. Evans. Unlucky for me, the new social worker thought it would be best if I stayed with Dad while they sorted through the evidence to find out what the deal was.

But then I remembered the evidence Janine got for me. I'd left her phone in my bedroom on my desk! If the social worker saw those, she would put two and two together! So I shouted about Dad dumpster-diving and that he wanted to frame us! I told everybody that I had proof upstairs on Janine's rainbow-kitty smart phone. Dad wasn't even fazed when I said that! I should have known something else was up.

When I got there, the phone was gone. Dad must have spotted it and seen the photos! He took the phone! That was that—we were sunk! Mr. Evans said that he'd counsel Janine if the cops could prove Dad's claims. Dad, as smooth and as sly as ever, convinced everyone that he'd watch over me and make sure I had a secure home and good, clean food. He'd won. Dad had beaten us.

I'm at his apartment now. He was only four blocks from our place the whole time. I'm writing this after an hour of "bonding" he made me do in front of the lady social worker, Mrs. McNeil. We played video games...a football video game. Ugh!

After that, I had to choke down that ashy-tasting "normal food". Mrs. McNeil stayed for dinner 'cause Dad invited her. He laid it on thick all evening. What a "great guy" my dad is. Chyeah, right! With dinner done, Dad's guest said good night, and I got immediately sent to bed. No practice today. No future. The only things I have now are my school books from my backpack and my diary.

Game over, man. Game over.

Tuesday

Sunny all day.

Breakfast: Oatmeal. Warm Milk. Fresh Juice.

Today's Record: Still no gaming!

Dad got me excused from school today. He called in and explained that there were domestic problems and that I needed to spend some time recovering with him. Of course, the school principal bought his baloney.

After one of the most tasteless, bland breakfasts I've ever had, he took me to the park for some outdoor father-son bonding. He made sure that Mrs. McNeil was there to witness me having "fun" and adjusting. Dad had a baseball, two gloves, and a football with him.

THE TORTURE BEGINS!

The feelings of dread on the drive up to the park could not possibly be described!

Mrs. McNeil was already at the park when Dad pulled up. His fake warm greeting got her to smile immediately. But when he opened my car door to let me out, he whispered, "Go ahead and act up in front of Mrs. McNeil, you little loser. I DARE you. It'll give me a reason to ship you off to military school! I don't need you around. I just need custody!"

FATHER'S DAY CARD MATERIAL, DAD IS NOT!

So that whole morning was basically a nightmare. Dad kept tossing the ball so I'd miss it. And I had to run around, as fast as my slow zombie kid legs could move me, and play along. I was stuck in his trap, man! If I made one wrong move, he'd have an excuse to ship me off to military school! And there's no telling if or when he's going to do that ANYWAY!

The one thing that kept bothering me all morning was not figuring out Dad's end game. I had to come up with a plan, and I think my idea was a good start.

On the way back to Dad's apartment, I noticed a gas station that had a bunch of beer advertisements plastered on its windows. Perfect! Dad loves his beers, and he always takes a nap after he's downed a few. As we came closer, I started coughing...loud! "Dad, can I have a soda? My throat's really dry." I could see him shaking his head to say no, just out of spite...but then he saw those beer ads!

"Actually, that's not a bad idea, Billy-boy! We've been playin' hard all morning! Let's quench some thirst!" Hook, line, and sinker!

Once home, I nursed my can of soda and watched a football game with Dad. He even got me to run to the fridge for another "cold one" every commercial break. At that point, I was more than willing to make sure he stayed nice and comfortable. After a while, he nodded off, and I started looking all around the apartment for a clue—anything that would tip me off to what Dad's game was. If I knew that, I could work on beating him at it!

Unfortunately...I got caught. Mission accomplished, but I messed up and got caught. He locked me in my room, and there was no way out! Dad said I was staying here until the morning, then the guys from the military academy would come to take me away. I had to find a way out of there...if there WAS a way out!

But I found out why Dad wants custody of me so bad: money. I should have known. His laptop computer had all the answers. I just needed to find the password. Then I just guessed "p.a.s.s.w.o.r.d.", and bingo, I was in. Some grownups need a reality check on how "clever" their security really is.

In Dad's computer was a file on a trust fund—MY trust fund! Dad had set it up to stash a ton of cash from when he was cheating on Wall Street. The courts couldn't find enough evidence to link my trust fund to his crimes, so it was still ripe for the plucking! That's what Dad wanted control over! The thing is, he can't get control until he's got official custody of me as my parent and guardian!

I got my backpack and I copied everything I could about the trust fund in the back of my notebook. But before I could power the computer down and get the heck out of there, Dad woke up and stared at me from the hallway. "You sneaky little loser!"

He grabbed me, took my notebook and threw it in the trash, then dragged me to my room and locked the door. "It doesn't matter what you know now, anyway. Tomorrow morning, I'll have control of that trust fund. That's when guys from the military academy are coming to drag you away, Billy-boy! You lose!" Then he laughed and went back to his drinking and his ball game!

The only thing I had was my diary...and my stomach rumbles. I hadn't had anything good to eat in a while, and that normal food and soda really did a number on my stomach. Then my stomach grumbled, and I had a great idea! It was then that I made my escape!

I'm bad! Bad to the bone! My zombie bones! Shwanzenheimer, Sylvester Malone, Mr. G, Chuck Maurice, Bruce Lu! Line 'em up. All the tough guys you can find. I bet not one of them can stack up to me!

Here's how my escape went down!

First, I scooted the chair next to my desk around, like I was moving around furniture. I had to make it sound like I was up to something dangerous. Then, when

I heard Dad wake up and scream for me to keep it quiet, I stood on my desk and did a belly flop onto the floor face down, making sure I yelped on the way down!

IF THERE WERE AN OLYMPIC MEDAL FOR PAINFULLY DIVING FACE-FIRST ONTO THE FLOOR...

I've got to admit, taking that belly flop was a painfully awful idea. Even with my dulled-down zombie nerves, it hurt. In retrospect, I could have just tossed something heavy on the floor to fake the sound of my impact. But, the next part was easy: playing dead!

Not moving, not even breathing that much for a loooooong time is something Mom discovered we could do. She uses that technique to pretend to be a tree. As silly as that sounds, the grackles in the backyard fall for that stunt every single time! That's how she got the meat for those "beak-fast" burritos!

All I had to do was wait in complete and utter silence. After a while, the suspense got to Dad, and he opened the door to check on me. Little did he know, with my butt facing the door, he was in just the right position for my cannon—my BUTT cannon! All I needed was for him to take a step closer and get into range!

JUST A LITTLE CLOSER....

Dad kicked my shoe hard, but that didn't matter. I knew he'd do that, and I kept playing 'possum! When I heard him swear, I knew I had fooled him into thinking I was hurt...maybe even DEAD! As he bent over to pick me up, he put his face just a foot away from my rear end, which was right where I wanted him. As I knew it wouldn't, my butt did NOT fail me!

I mentioned before how my fart could be classified as a weapon of mass destruction, didn't I? Well, this time, Dad was the target, and he was utterly destroyed! As the wood panel floor vibrated from the shockwave, I almost felt sorry for him...almost. When I turned to look at the results, I could see his limbs already deprived of strength, growing lifeless and limp. He stumbled back and splatted hard on the floor face up. Bullseye!

I knew I had to work fast after that. The air was cleaner near the floor where he lay, and he'd be coming around again soon. So, I went for the trash where he threw my notebook, then tried the door, but it was padlocked with a bicycle chain! Any other middle schooler would have been trapped like a rat...but not me! Especially since I know how great my chompers work!

THIS IS ACTUALLY AN EXAGGERATION. IT TOOK A FEW GNAWS...

With the door unlocked, I ran out of the apartment building as fast as my lethargic, slow zombie feet could carry me. From then on, it was a race against time! I hoped my gas would give me a big enough head start.

Unfortunately, it didn't. Thanks to my turtle-slow running speed, Dad had plenty of time to wake up and figure out what happened. He was furious once his head cleared, too. There's nothing a cheating sore loser like Dad hates more than being beaten despite all his cheating.

I was two blocks away from home when I heard him running up behind me. I remember thinking I was done for. Even if I yelled for help, he could make it look like I was just being disobedient, especially if he took my notebook first! He could charm his way out of almost anything! The next thing I knew, I was being knocked over. "You little punk! You thought that was funny!? HUH!?" He raised his fist to hit me. Man, I hate bullies!

But that's all he did. The police siren didn't come on until after they stopped the cars. BOTH of the cars! Out stepped two policemen, Mom, Mr. Evans, Larry and Janine. They were all on their way to Dad's apartment! Man, was Dad surprised! I was too! I didn't get what was going on until Janine showed me her rainbow-kitty smart phone. She'd found it!

It seems Dad had tossed the phone into the bushes out back, not knowing that Larry could help Janine find it just by tracking it with GPS and then calling Janine's number to pinpoint its location! The pics on that cell phone and the discovery of those garbage-filled duffle bags in the dumpster behind the apartment was all the evidence Mr. Evans needed to clear Mom's name. My notes on that trust fund scam were all the COPS needed to haul Dad away for good! Winning!!!

So I'm back home safe and sound with Mom. We all celebrated by going out to eat at a restaurant. But Mom was quick on her feet and texted that she wanted to go French for some escargot. How about that? Mom found a zombie-friendly eatery!

That dinner kind of inspired Mom to learn more about world cuisines and which ones can be stuffed in the fridge to keep up appearances. The "beak-fast" burritos are still there, wrapped in tin foil. But with the French and Indian "gross" meals up front on the rack, no one would bother to go deeper into the fridge for the homemade dishes. Way to go, Mom!

FROM NOW ON, OUR MEALS AREN'T GROSS...THEY'RE "EXOTIC"!

Too bad about the trust fund, though. It's tied up in the courts until they can find the rightful owners of the money Dad stole. Easy come, easy go, I guess. I'm really just glad to have my life back...and my Mom.

The only thing that's bugging me is Janine and Larry's weird fascination with the pamphlets Mr. Epstein made from my comics. I missed school today, so I really don't have any firsthand accounts of what the reaction was, but Janine and Larry sure seem to be getting a kick out of them. Hopefully, it's nothing to worry about. It's not like some dumb history comic I made could derail my pro-gamer career plans as hard as Dad sending me to military school might have done.

Right?

BONUS LEVEL ENTRY

I never know how something I do is going to affect the analysis data for my perfect gaming conditions, so for the sake of completeness, I'm including copies of the art I did for Janine.

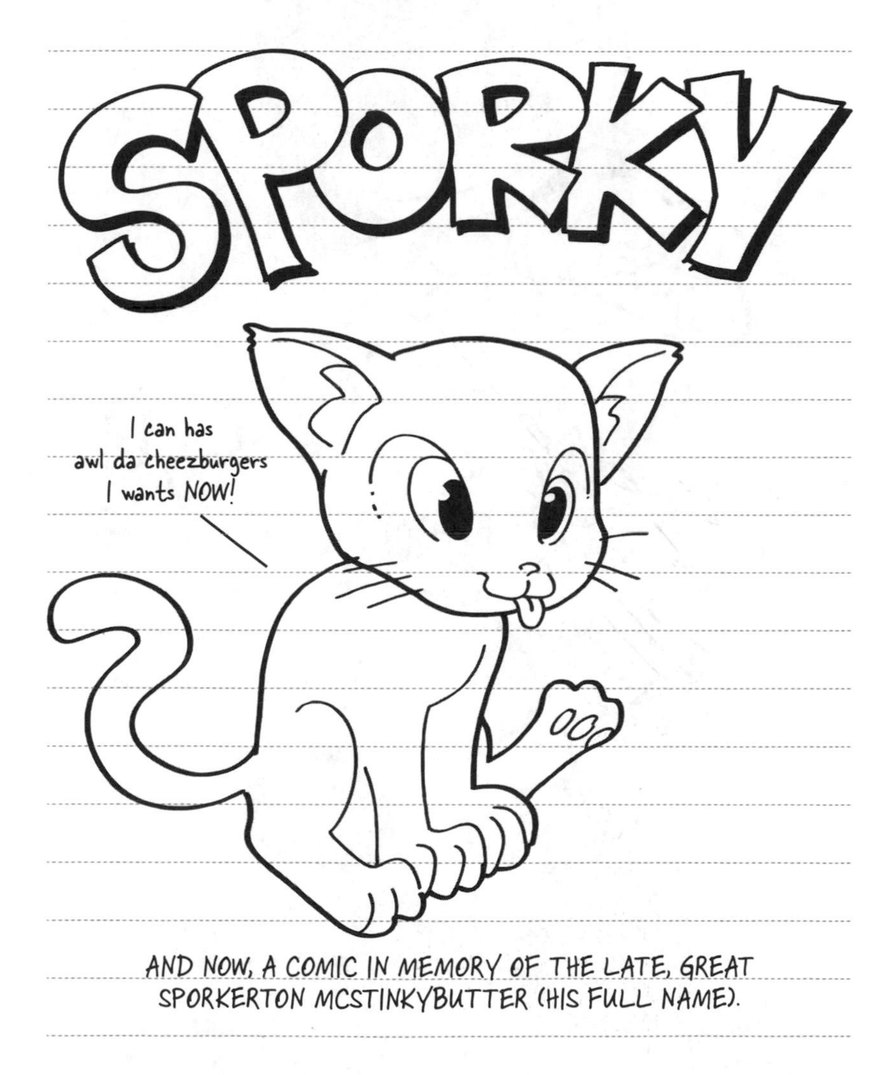

AND NOW, A COMIC IN MEMORY OF THE LATE, GREAT SPORKERTON MCSTINKYBUTTER (HIS FULL NAME).

SPORKY WAS A QUIRKY KITTY, A TRAIT THAT JANINE LOVED FROM THE VERY FIRST TIME THEY MET!

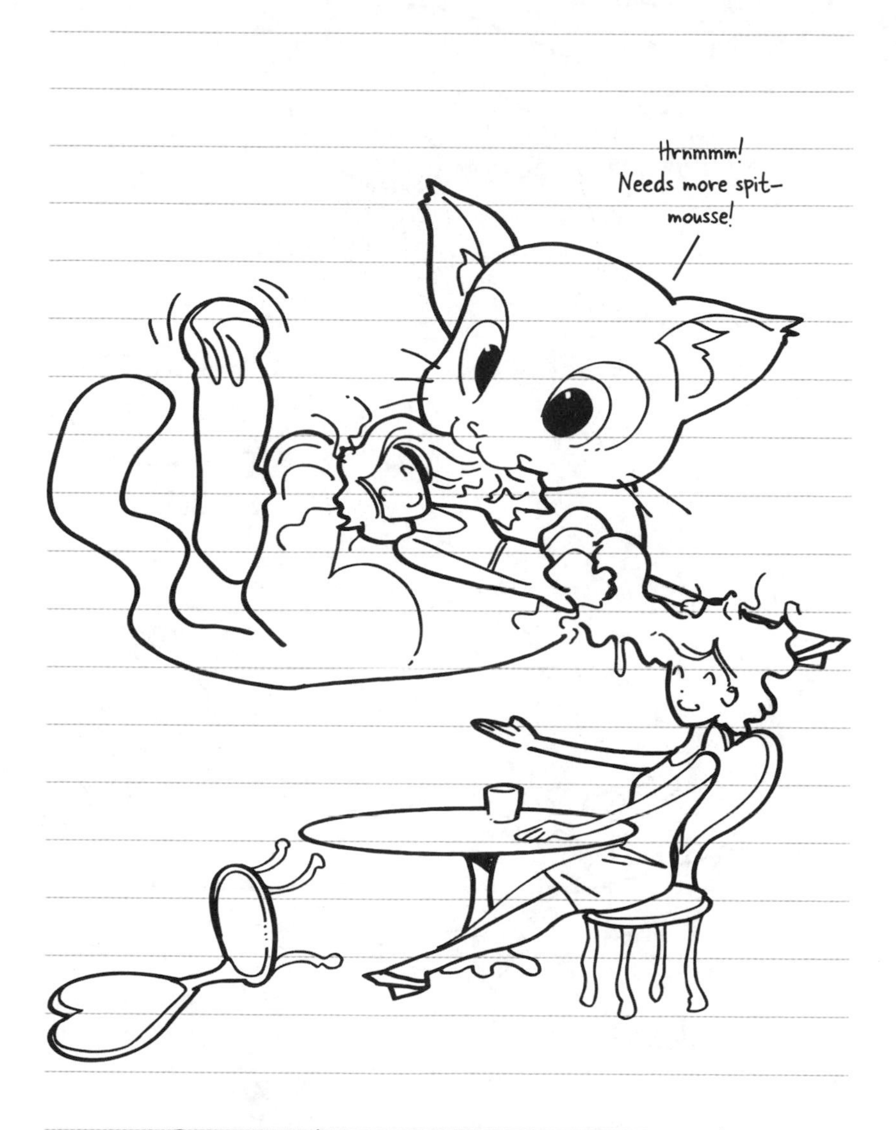

BUT SPORKY WAS A HELPFUL LITTLE DICKENS!
HE EVEN HELPED JANINE STYLE HER DOLLS' HAIR!

SPORKY MADE SURE THE LEFTOVER
CHINESE TAKE-OUT NEVER WENT TO WASTE!

AND, SOMEHOW, THE MORE YOU FED HIM,
THE FEWER BONES SPORKY SEEMED TO HAVE...

SPORKY LOVED TO WARM HIS KITTY BUNS BY THE FIRE ON COLD WINTER NIGHTS...WHICH WAS KIND OF DANGEROUS WHEN YOU REMEMBER THAT SPORKY WAS ONE GASSY KITTY!

SPORKY HELPED AROUND THE NEIGHBORHOOD, TOO! IF THERE WAS A NASTY LITTLE MOUSE OR RATTY LITTLE RAT AROUND, SOMEHOW OR ANOTHER, SPORKY WOULD END UP CLOBBERING IT... IF ONLY JUST BECAUSE HE HAD TO TAKE SO MANY REST BREAKS!

HOW MANY CATS DO YOU KNOW THAT ARE WILLING TO WALK A MILE IN YOUR SHOES?

AND LET'S NOT FORGET HOW SPORKY FOUND NEW, EXCITING USES FOR CURTAINS AND BLINDS!

SPORKY IS GONE, BUT NOT FORGOTTEN. AND HE'LL BE WATCHING OVER YOU. BUT HOPEFULLY NOT *DIRECTLY* OVER YOU.